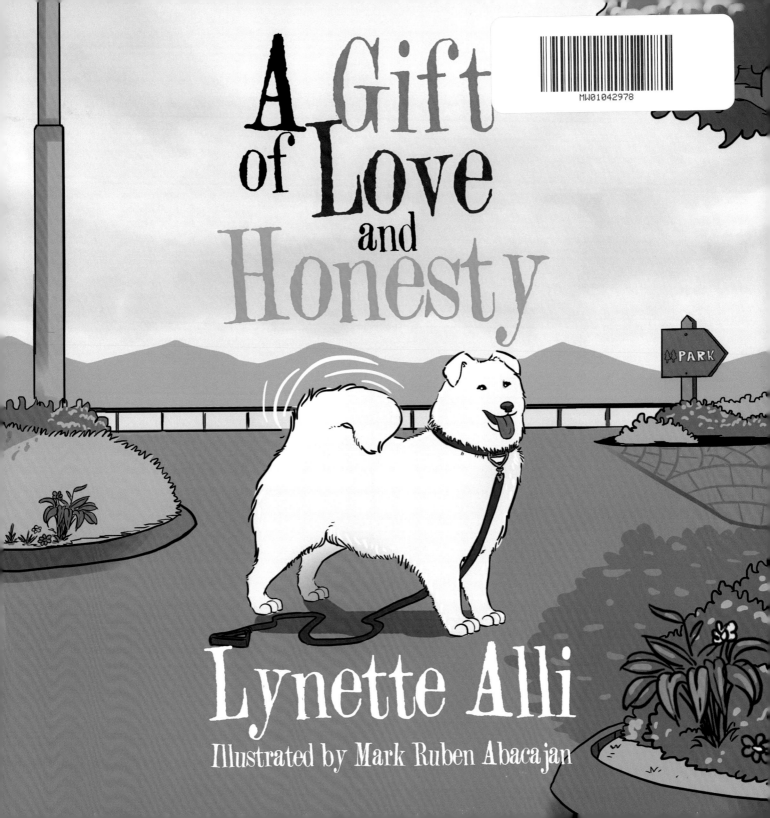

A Gift of Love and Honesty

Lynette Alli

Illustrated by Mark Ruben Abacajan

PARK

Print information available on the last page

Rev. date: 1/12/2018

To order additional copies of this book, contact:
Xlibris
1-888-795-4274
www.Xlibris.com
Orders@Xlibris.com

For all the children of the world

Mistakes are part of growing up,
and they can be corrected.

Although children have little minds, they
are the world's biggest thinkers.

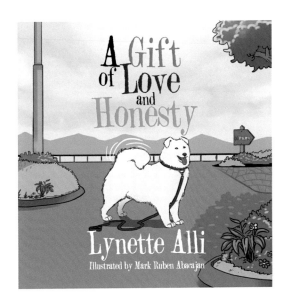

Sincere thanks to my husband, Akbar;
daughter, Nezie; and son-in-law, Raymond,
for their help and support.

Mr. Small lived in a quiet neighborhood in a small house.

He drove a small car and even wore a small hat.

But his new dog was not so small.

Mr. Small was known to almost everyone because he told the same story about his new dog.

He named her Angel, and he loved her very much from her giant paws to her wet kisses.

He could speak for hours about his best friend.

Whenever he was walking Angel and someone stopped to pet his dog or made a comment, he would start to tell the same story.

He would have a bright smile on his face whenever he told the story.

Mr. Small explained, "I named her Angel because she was given to me by a little girl whose brother made a mistake."

A long time ago, before he had Angel, Mr. Small had a small dog named Buddy. Buddy had a beautiful black leather leash.

Mr. Small and Buddy would go for walks for hours at a time.

Mr. Small would sit on his favorite bench while Buddy rested.

But as the years passed, Buddy slowed down.

Walks got shorter, and naps got longer.

Then one day Buddy didn't walk anymore.

After Buddy was gone, Mr. Small went for walks alone.

He couldn't let go of the leash.

He sat on a bench in Buddy's favorite park and gazed off.

One afternoon, Mr. Small fell asleep on the bench in the park.

He was awakened by the sound of a dog barking.

He thought Buddy was back but realized it was a dream.

Feeling sad, Mr. Small went home.

When Mr. Small got home, he realized he must have left Buddy's leash on the bench in the park.

Luckily, when he returned to the park, it was still there.

As Mr. Small was leaving the park, a little girl came over with her parents.

Her name was Pari, and her parents were Mr. and Mrs. Verma.

She told Mr. Small her brother, Raj, took his dog's leash and brought it home.

Their parents told him to return it, which he did.

Pari told Mr. Small she was sorry for what Raj had done and that she knew how much the leash meant to him.

Mr. Small said to Pari, "Little girl, you are very honest, and I know, you and your brother are sorry for what he did."

A few days later, Mr. Small was sitting on the bench as usual in the park, holding his Buddy's leash.

The Verma family came back to the park to meet Mr. Small.

Raj looked worried, but Pari was smiling. She was carrying a beautiful big white dog in her arms.

Pari told Mr. Small her brother was scared and ashamed for stealing the dog's leash.

He wrote about his mistake in his class journal but was still feeling guilty whenever he went to the park.

Raj told Mr. Small he was sorry for what he had done.

Mr. Small said, "Little boy, I am very proud of you for returning the leash and for writing about what you did in your class journal."

Raj felt happy that Mr. Small was not angry.

Pari handed Mr. Small the dog and said, "Sir, this is a present for you so you can use your dog leash again."

Mr. Small was touched by the honesty and bravery of the children. He smiled, thanking them.

That evening, Raj hugged Pari because she understood his guilt and she was the one who suggested getting a dog for Mr. Small's leash.

Raj also told Pari what she did for him was great and he would always remember it.

Pari then told her brother she shared his pain in silence and thought of a way to help him and Mr. Small.

Mr. Small had a new best friend and used his black leather leash again.

Raj was happy because of his sister's bravery, love, and care for him and Mr. Small.

That same evening, Raj thanked his parents for the lessons they taught him and his sister.

"If its' not yours, do not take it." And this was what he wrote in his class journal.

Mrs. Verma turned to Pari and said, "Your name, Pari, means 'fairy.'"

Pari said, "Really? I am glad my name is Pari and my powers helped Raj!"

They all laughed.

Mr. Small was happy when he went for his walks with Angel and his old dog leash.

He remembered the moment when he got his new dog and thought an angel visited him in the park.

He learnt later that Pari's name meant "fairy" and thought to himself, *What a blessing!*

Mr. Small used Buddy's leash for Angel. He would cherish the memories of Buddy, but he loved Angel very much.

This was the story he would tell over and over again–about his happy moments with his best friend, Angel, and about Pari, the "little fairy girl."

A Gift of Love and Honesty

This is a sequel to Seven Little Words in a Journal.

Lynette Alli was born in Guyana, South America, where she was a teacher for twelve years. She now resides in Ontario, Canada, with her husband. She is also the author of My Grandmother's Basket, A Message from Allan, and Seven Little Words in a Journal.

Mr. Small said, "Little boy, I am very proud of you for returning the leash and for writing what you did in your class journal."

Xlibris

TADEO TURTLE

Children's
Activities
Included

WRITTEN AND ILLUSTRATED BY
JANIS COX